Hey! What's that Sound?

Veronika Martenova Charles

Stoddart

Text and illustrations copyright © 1994
by Veronika Martenova Charles

First published in 1994 by
Stoddart Publishing Co. Limited
34 Lesmill Road
Toronto, Canada
M3B 2T6
(416) 445-3333

Canadian Cataloguing in Publication Data

Charles, Veronika Martenova
Hey! What's that sound?

ISBN 0-7737-2841-4
ISBN 0-7737-5702-3 (pb)

I. Title.

PS8555.TT42TT4   jC813'.54   C94-930296-1
PZ7.C53TTe 1994

Book design: Kathryn Cole and Veronika Martenova Charles

Printed in Hong Kong

For Margaret and Jenny

I hear the *telephone*.

It sounds like…?

**My mom says Aunt Minnie is coming.
Aunt Minnie is funny. I like her a lot!**

I hear a *siren*.

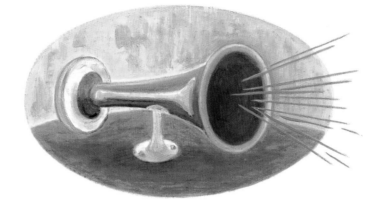

It sounds like…?

Aunt Minnie is here in her big red car.

I hear the *doorbell.*

It sounds like…?

Aunt Minnie is at the door.
She has presents for us!

I hear *kissing*.

It sounds like…?

Aunt Minnie is happy to see us.
She likes to kiss and hug.

I hear the *kettle*.

It sounds like…?

My mom makes tea for Aunt Minnie.
She says, "Let's have it in the garden."

I hear *drinking*.

It sounds like…?

Aunt Minnie is sipping her tea.

I hear *crunching*.

It sounds like…?

Dylan is chewing
his cookie from Aunt Minnie.

I hear singing...
Aunt Minnie is teaching
Dylan to sing.

I hear clapping...

Mom joins in the song.

I hear banging...

I join in too.

I hear chirping...

Even the birds are singing.

Oh! I hear a *clatter*...

The cat jumps at the birds.
The tray falls off the table.
The honey spills all over the dog.
What a sticky mess!

I hear *barking*…
The dog is chasing the cat.

I hear *huffing and puffing*…
Aunt Minnie is chasing the dog.

I hear *laughter*…
Mom laughs hard
as she fills the wash tub.

I hear *splashing*.

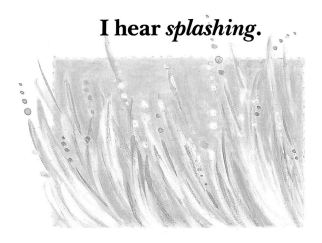

It sounds like…?

I hear *screaming*.

It sounds like…?

Aunt Minnie is soaking wet.

I hear the *wind*.

It sounds like…?

I hear *raindrops*.

They sound like…?

We all say,
"Hurry! Run inside!"

I hear a *crash*!

It sounds like…?

**The flower pot fell over.
"It's all right," Aunt Minnie says.
"It was an accident."**

**My mom thinks it's time for dogs
and children to have a nap.**

I hear *knocking*.

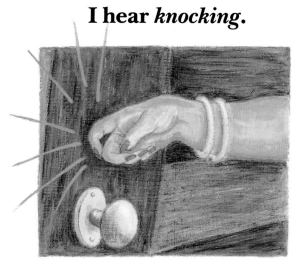

It sounds like...?

Aunt Minnie is here to read me a book.

Hey! What's that sound? *Snoring*?

It sounds like…?

**Aunt Minnie's had too much excitement.
She needs a nap too.
I'll make it quiet for her.**

I hear *silence*.

It sounds like…